Carolrhoda Books
A division of Lerner Publishing Group, Inc.
241 First Avenue North
Minneapolis, MN 55401 USA

For reading levels and more information, look up this title at www.lernerbooks.com.

Designed by Laura Otto Rinne.
Main body text set in Burin Roman. Typeface provided by Monotype.
The illustrations in this book were created using colored pencil.

Library of Congress Cataloging-in-Publication Data

Names: Hosford, Kate. | Swiatkowska, Gabi, illustrator.
Title: How the queen found the perfect cup of tea / by Kate Hosford ;
illustrated by Gabi Swiatkowska.
Description: Minneapolis, MN : Carolrhoda Picture Books, 2016. | Summary: A
pampered queen sets out in a hot air balloon with her butler, James, in search of the
perfect cup of tea and after stopping in Japan, India, and England, she returns home
knowing exactly what she has been missing.
Identifiers: LCCN 2014035894 | ISBN 9781467739047 (lb : alk. paper)
Subjects: | CYAC: Tea—Fiction. | Kings, queens, rulers, etc.—Fiction. |
Voyages and travels—Fiction. | Behavior—Fiction.
Classification: LCC PZ7.H79313 Ho 2016 | DDC [E]—dc23

LC record available at https://lccn.loc.gov/2014035894

Manufactured in the United States of America
1-38716-20632-7/8/2016

How the QUEEN FOUND the PERFECT CUP of TEA

Kate Hosford

Illustrated by
Gabi Swiatkowska

Carolrhoda Books • Minneapolis

To my parents, who always make
everyone feel welcome in their home
—K.H.

To Kate H., who deals with all sorts
of royal personages daily
—G.S.

Every morning when the Queen woke up, two maids dressed her, two more styled her hair, and the butler made her tea. Each day, she sipped her tea, alone. And each day, her tea started to taste a bit worse. Finally, she could stand it no longer.

"James," she yelled,

"This tea is horrible!"

"Oh dear," said James. "Too much sugar? Too little milk?"

"Too much talking!" said the Queen. "I must find the perfect cup of tea. Stop slouching and get me my coat!"

"Yes, Your Majesty," said James.

They floated over hilltops, meadows, and seas.

"Land there,"
the Queen commanded.

The Queen walked with her nose in the
air and addressed a young girl.
"Who are you, pray tell?"

"I'm Noriko," said the girl, "and you're just in time.
My kitties would like to snuggle."

"James, tell her I do not snuggle," said the Queen.

"Her Majesty does not snuggle,"
said James.
"Well then, it's time she tried,"
said Noriko.

"Oh my," said the Queen. "That was rather strenuous."

"Might I have a cup of tea?"

"Certainly," said Noriko. "You can help me make it."
She took the Queen by the hand and led her to the kitchen.
The Queen helped by finding the faucet and turning it on.
Then she observed carefully while Noriko did the rest.

gather

heat water

sift powder

whisk until frothy

add water

serve immediately

They sat down to tea and talked until they had each
finished one cup. When they were done, the Queen arose.
"That was lovely indeed. Thank you ever so much. I must
be off now. Ta-ta."

"Has Your Majesty found the **perfect** cup of tea?" said James.

"Not yet," said the Queen, "but that cup was rather good. Onward, James!"

They floated over forests, villages, and fields.

"Land there," the Queen commanded.

The Queen walked with her nose in the air and addressed a young boy. "Who are you, pray tell?"

"I'm Sunil," said the boy. "And you're just in time to dribble."

"James, tell him I **do not** dribble," said the Queen.

"Her Majesty does not dribble," said James.

"Well then, it's time she tried," said Sunil.

"Oh my," said the Queen.
"That was rather vigorous."

"Might I have a cup of tea?"

"Definitely," said Sunil. "You
can help me make it." He took the
Queen by the hand and led her to
the kitchen.

The Queen helped by finding
a faucet, turning it on, and filling
the kettle.

Then she observed carefully
while Sunil did the rest.

gather

chop ginger

combine, minus
honey

boil

lower heat,
simmer

strain, add honey

serve

They sat down to tea and talked until they had each finished two cups. When they were done, the Queen arose. "That was lovely indeed. Thank you ever so much. I must be off now. Ta-ta."

"Has Your Majesty found the perfect cup of tea?" said James.

"Not yet," said the Queen, "but those cups were rather good. Onward, James!"

They floated over mountains, valleys, and lakes.

"Land there,"
the Queen commanded.

James rolled out the red carpet. The Queen walked
with her nose in the air and addressed a young girl.

"Who are you, pray tell?"

"I'm Rana," said the girl. "And you're just in time to dance."

"James, tell her I **do not** dance," said the Queen.

"Her Majesty does not dance," said James.
"Well then, it's time she tried," said Rana.

"Oh my," said the Queen.
"That was rather marvelous!"

"Might I have a cup of tea?"

"Surely," said Rana. "You can help me make it." She took the Queen by the hand and led her to the kitchen.

The Queen helped by finding the faucet, turning it on, filling the kettle, and boiling the water. Then she observed carefully while Rana did the rest.

gather

fill

rinse tea leaves

add leaves

stack and
boil

pour,

lower heat, steep

combine brew and water

serve

They sat down to tea and talked until they had each finished three cups. After they were done, the Queen arose. "That was lovely indeed. Thank you ever so much. I must be off now. Ta-ta."

"Has Your Majesty found the **perfect cup of tea**?" said James.
"Not yet," said the Queen. "But now I know where it is.

Home, James!"

When the Queen got back to her castle, she
called James to make some special deliveries.

Your presence
is requested by
Her Majesty the Queen
at a Royal Tea Party
Saturday at 3:00 PM.

On Saturday, the Queen woke up,

styled her own hair, and dressed herself.

When it was time for the party, the Queen went to the royal kitchen,

found the faucet,

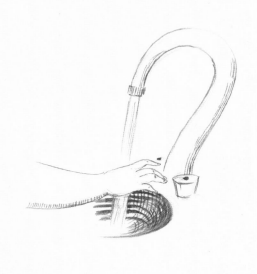

turned it on,

filled the kettle,

set the kettle on the stove,

boiled the water,   and then brewed the tea.

She even set out milk and sugar.

James rolled out the red carpet and greeted each guest.

Sunil arrived first,
followed by Noriko
and Rana.

When everyone was assembled, James blew his bugle.

"The Queen has an announcement," he said.

The guests grew quiet.

"I have discovered the secret to the perfect cup of tea," said the Queen.

"First, you must make the tea yourself.

Then you must share it with others.

Milk and sugar are optional."

"Precisely," said Noriko.

"Exactly," said Sunil.

"Absolutely," said Rana.

The Queen was so busy serving tea that she forgot to put her nose in the air. This caused her crown to wobble just a bit.

"Come join us," said Noriko.

"That would be lovely indeed," said the Queen.

Everyone sat down to tea, where they talked and laughed

and drank cup after cup until the whole teapot was empty.

Author's Note

I have always loved how a cup of tea can bring people together. I once spent an afternoon drinking tea with a Turkish family I had met on top of a mountain. We talked for hours, although I did not speak Turkish and they did not speak English. I'm not sure how we understood each other, but perhaps that is the magic of tea. Around the world, drinking tea gives us the chance to sit down, relax, and connect with other people.

How did tea become such a wildly popular, global drink? People in ancient China began to sip tea around four thousand years ago, at first as medicine and eventually as an everyday drink. Centuries later, it caught on in other parts of the world. Japanese monks who had studied in China introduced tea to their own culture. In the 1600s, traders from the British East India Company probably brought Chinese tea to Britain (now the United Kingdom). In northern India, people had long brewed local tea leaves. But by the mid-1800s, India was under British rule, and Indian plantation workers produced huge amounts of tea to meet British demand. Soon this energizing drink was popular throughout India as well. In Turkey, tea became an essential part of the culture in the last hundred years, after coffee became more expensive. Around the globe, many cultures have woven tea into daily life, in their own unique ways.

When I decided to write this book, I imagined a spoiled queen drinking tea by herself, and growing more miserable every day. I knew right away that she would have to go on an adventure to find the secret to the perfect cup of tea, and that her story could celebrate the rich variety of tea traditions around the world.

The children she meets in Japan, India, and Turkey teach her how to make tea, and also teach her to be more open-minded, independent, and generous. The Queen learns that no matter which kind of tea you drink, the perfect cups are the ones you make yourself and share with others. Sometimes, this simple act of kindness may even be enough to start a friendship.